Grow it!

illustrated by Georgie Birkett

Look at me! I'm on the compost heap!

Can we grow some of these seeds?

First, we'll fill up the tray. Spread it out.

These seeds are tiny. Can I push them in?

You need to water the seedlings. Oh no!

I'm all wet! Now you'll grow, just like a plant!

Why are we planting these outside?

I'll sprinkle these seeds on the soil.

How much water do these plants need?

My hands are muddy. This water's cold!

I'll pull out the weeds. We don't want them.

Should I take them to the compost heap?

Wow! Are the sunflowers taller than me now?

The tomatoes are heavy. I'll tie them up.

We need a rest after all that hard work!

Phew! This pumpkin makes a great seat.

So many tomatoes! They're really juicy.

Would you like these? Yes, let's swap!

Here I am! These beans are crunchy.

Are the lettuces ready? Plenty to share!

Home-grown salad. Nothing tastes better!

What will we grow to eat next year?

One day, I'll be as tall as these!